ENDORSEMENTS

"I always loved getting a new song from Rock Killough. To hear Rock sing the songs he wrote is like having a direct connection to his soul. His writing and reading of short stories is just an extension of this very gifted artist. The soul of Rock is pure GOLD."

~ Duane Allen
The Oak Ridge Boys

"A master wordsmith whose lyrics and stories pull you in like you are riding shotgun. Rock Killough is a true southern treasure. Hop in and enjoy the ride!"

~ Steve Norman
Probate Judge, Butler County Alabama (ret)

"I've been listening and enjoying Rock's stories and musings for the 40 years we've traveled the roads playing our songs. Some are funny, some thoughtful, but all are from the heart."

~ Sonny Throckmorton
Hall of Fame Songwriter

"I have been a fan of Rock Killough's songwriting since I first heard the magnificence of *'House at the End of the Road'* many years ago. This new collection of stories Rock tells us from his life growing up in the country takes me back to my own childhood's front porch when life was a lot more simple and a lot more easy to understand. Surely Rock's life has been and still is a beautiful song."

~ Buddy Cannon
Hall of Fame Songwriter and Producer

"From *'Take Jesus As Your Lawyer'* to *'Where Can I Surrender'* to *'Still Loving You'* to *'The House at the end of the Road,'* Rock has always written thought provoking music. In his vintage years, his musings from the front porch have always stirred beautiful images and points of view that I might have not considered before, but have always entertained! You will enjoy this collection!"

~ Debbie Phillips
(Mrs. Bum Phillips)

ROCK KILLOUGH'S
FRONT PORCH
NO. 2018586
1ST EDITION
TEXAS, U.S.A
STORIES

This book is protected by copyright laws of the United States of America. This book may not be copied or reprinted for commercial gain or profit. The use of short quotations or occasional page copying for personal or group study is permitted and encouraged. Permission will be granted upon request.

Scripture taken from the New King James Version®.
Copyright © 1982 by Thomas Nelson.
Used by permission. All rights reserved.

GOD MANIFEST PUBLISHING

www.GodManifestPublishing.com

This book and all other God Manifest Publishing and God Manifest Publishing Fiction
books are available on Amazon.com.

Creative direction by Jonnathan Zin Truong
Cover designed by Donald Tuangtuang
Interior designed by Uyen Vu
Photography by Rock Killough, Kathryn Killough Stengel, and istockphoto.com
Photo credit, page 54: Tamy and Alaina McDonald
For more information on foreign distributors, email publishers@godmanifestpublishing.com

Paperback: ISBN: 978-1-7340556-7-2
Hardcover: ISBN: 979-8-9857412-0-9
eBook: ISBN: 978-1-7340556-8-9
Audio: ISBN: 978-1-7340556-9-6

Printed in the United States of America.
Copyright © 2022 Rock Killough
All rights reserved.

ROCK KILLOUGH

DEDICATION

This little collection is dedicated to:

my niece, Kathryn Killough Stengel, who encouraged me
and assisted me in getting the stories recorded,

my friend, Mrs. Debbie Phillips, who referred me to
God Manifest Publishing,

and my generous and patient friends and family
who footed the bill.

TABLE OF CONTENTS

FOREWORD   By Rex Anderson

The front porch of Charlie Budd's Place, a hand-crafted home located at the edge of about twenty acres of working farmland, is Rock Killough's favorite stage these days. For a man who has stood on so many platforms, who has made a living and passed a life entertaining the masses from a raised dais, there is a gentle irony that his latest stage plays to the fewest chairs. When he plays guitar, he plays mostly now for himself. When he talks, he talks largely to his dog, Tater. When he converses, he converses mostly in the silent back and forth of friends in communion between himself and his Creator. When he gazes out across the room, his bright lights are the sunrise and the sunset, his bartenders now the sure slow movement of the seasons, and his favorite applause the sound of rain on his metal roof.

Rock told me stories a few years back about his uncle, who was a bootlegger—a good one, according to Rock, and one who went through all the trials and rewards commonly associated with such characters. He hid from the revenuers, he bested the competition, and he cultivated steady and serious customers. I don't know whether Rock counts his uncle among his personal heroes or even as any kind of role model, but I remember being struck at the time by how much Rock knew about the art and science of making whiskey.

In examining the process, it's not difficult to lay this bootlegger metaphor over Rock, over his life, over his habits of living. Brittanica defines the process of distillation as "conversion of a liquid into a vapor that is condensed back into liquid form." If our numbered days are liquid when they are passed to us at birth, if they vaporize as we live them, then, if we are so inclined—particularly in our later years—we are able to catch and savor the distilled essence of those vaporized days as memories, as relationships, as sweet moments to be rolled around the palette, to be tested and tasted and treasured over and again.

I could wear this metaphor out with Rock. He has crafted a life, and a living, from burning through and collecting the vapor of his days in an age when the larger portion of humanity seldom achieves temperature. He has drunk deeply of both the process and the product. He has become a master at describing the flavor for others, in handing the clues to our own hazy lives to us in a form we can understand, can hum, can even sing to ourselves when we're all alone.

For me, Rock's magic is in taking the everyday and making it transcendent. He knows he has the greatness of God within him, he knows this life is work, and he is not afraid to confront the ways he has failed. In my opinion, this alone is all the work anyone needs to do in a well-lived life. But Rock has done something else: he has set his efforts to music and poetry, to rhyme and melody, for most of his life. He has shaped these everyman struggles into songs we can listen to, and sing, and think about, and sip on over and over in our own efforts to make sense of our lives. And whether he ever knew any of us personally, all of us who love Rock have counted him as our friend because of these tools, these songs, which he has given us.

Now, on the sparse stage of Charlie Budd's Place in the sharp contours of his beloved northern Alabama, he has mostly laid down his music. He no longer feels the obligation to make words rhyme or even to fit an obvious pattern. He writes without filters on his heart or his mind. I can hear the songwriter's cadence and melody in his stories, and I feel sure you will too. But more, I recognize in these words the transcendent chords of a life at rest, the unassuming artistry of one who freely distills what the days hath brought, who drinks it, who tells us how it tastes, how it feels, and, as ever, encourages us to join him in savoring the heady spirits of all our lives.

MORNING

Like a cat, dawn comes creeping silently across the cornfield, sneaking up through the pines. The coming of the light, like a bugle call, is reveille to my little world.

Up rises the twitter of birds while hungry cows across the road mournfully moo their hungry impatience. Gliding quietly as predator drones, crows materialize out of the sun to check the corn while ravenous Japanese beetles buzz in the garden. Life has awakened around me like a mini-Creation: the sunlight pushing back the darkness and stirring life to action.

Maybe it's my age. Maybe it's the serenity of this little spot. I don't know. What I do know is that I can watch the sun break the darkness and smell the honeysuckle and privet from the porch.

In moments like this, sitting on the swing, watching the sunrise, and listening to the critters beginning to stir, I feel like my little world exists in some magical isolation. A world apart, encapsulated from the press of passing time. I feel joy, awed by a sense of flowing with time, and, for a moment, completely absorbed, suspended in the here and now: a heartbeat of not being aware and feeling the presence of the Almighty.

The message is clear to me. Even when depressing. Even when painful. Even at the end ... Life is a gift! Unwrap it and enjoy every minute you have left.

COFFEE IN THE MORNING

I've got to have a cup of coffee in the morning! My pumps won't come up to pressure until I have one.

When I was a kid, sometimes me and Mama would go out to Midway and spend the weekend with Mamaw and Papa Gene. Waking up in the morning at first light to Mamaw creeping around in the kitchen with the smell of her "Luzianne" chicory coffee brewing is a memory that remains strong.

Even today, the smell of coffee brewing takes me up like a cartoon character, floating on the aroma and drifting toward the coffee pot. Mama fixed my cup when I was a boy. She sweetened milk with sugar and put in just enough coffee to tint the milk to a light tan. And just like that, I was having coffee with Mama and Daddy. It was important!

All the adults around me drank it and seemed deeply satisfied, with an "Ahhh" after the first sip. Of course, that made me and every other kid want to partake. Even after I got grown, however, I still didn't care for it without milk and sugar. Later on at the hunting camp, sitting around the fire, groaning and moaning with the others that whiskey wouldn't let sleep, I learned to drink it black. This solidified its position in my life.

Now, when I sit on the porch in the stillness of the early morning, the sun seems to linger behind the trees until I have a cup of coffee. The first sip perfects the whole scene. It sort of raises me up, as the sun raises up the hum of life when it lifts the darkness.

Sometimes, at sunrise, I become absorbed, overcome by the beauty and the thrill of living. Off in my world, drifting and dreaming, I feel as though I'm sitting on the porch with the Good Lord, having coffee and watching the breaking dawn.

Well, the sun is up and so is my first cup. My pumps are coming online, so I'm going in to get that second cup and bring them on up to motivating pressure. I've got to pick peas and I need all the motivating I can get. Hmmm ... maybe I'll have three cups. The peas ain't going anywhere.

I love coffee in the morning. Don't you?

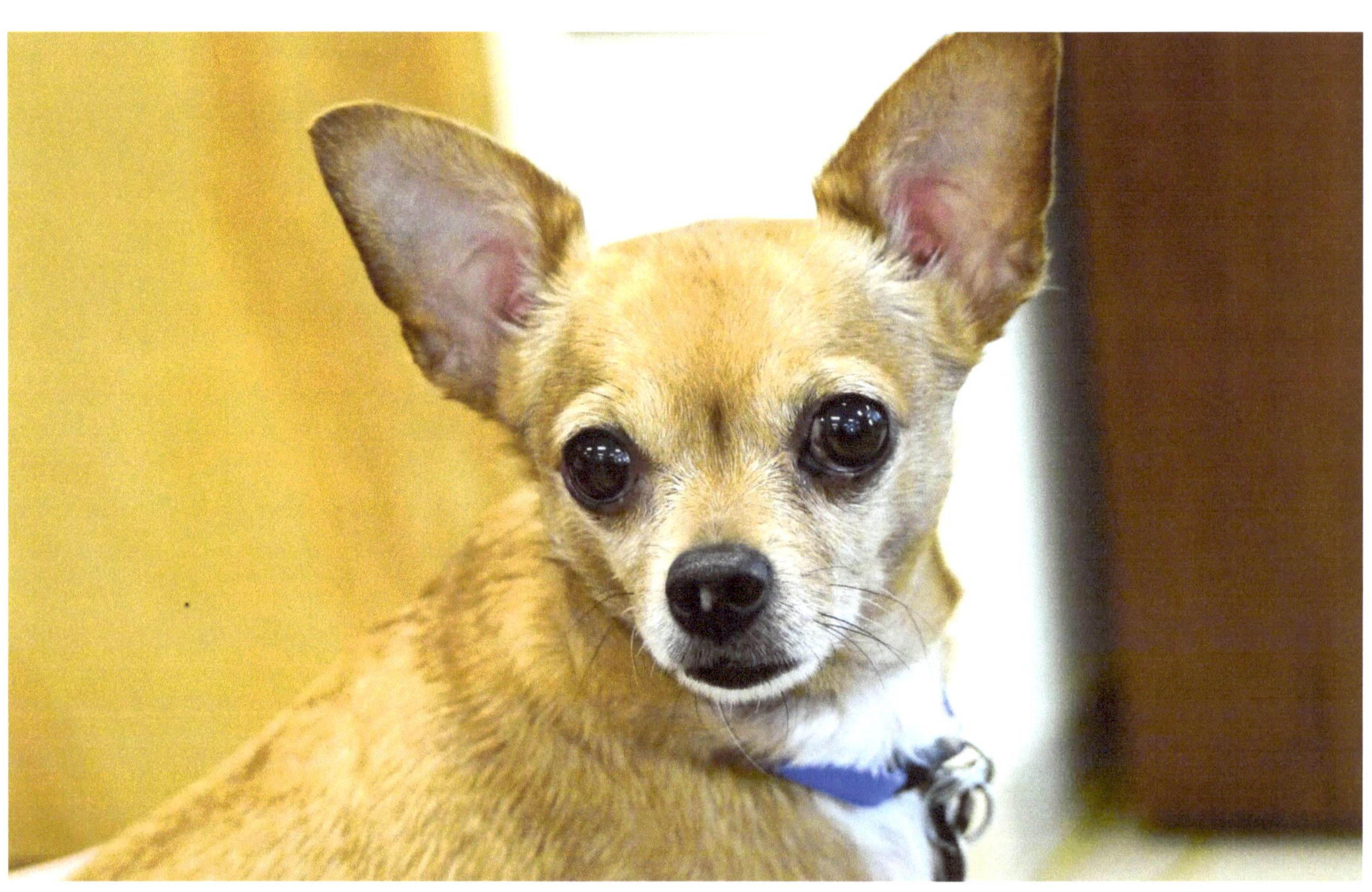

HONKYTONKISH

Tater, eating breakfast this morning. I know! It looks as though he's eating off a barroom floor. The bleak morning light pouring through the open door, the red glow of neon from the Marlboro sign, and the dingy carpet all indicate that he's in a den of iniquity.

My cabin reflects my comfort zone. I've been in houses that looked sterile as banks, some neat and clean as churches, some stuffed and organized like museums, and one or two absolute palaces. Most of them felt, well … sort of cold.

I've lived pretty much an unadorned life, preferring blue jeans and T-shirts to suits and ties. I'm more comfortable in a honkytonk than I am in a big church. It's not that I don't believe in our Heavenly Father or the saving power of Christ Jesus. It's just that churches these days feel cold, almost like the congregation is paying lip service to love.

Putting aside the craziness and anger that alcohol brings to people who overindulge, there is a warmness and genuine camaraderie in a honkytonk that is lacking in the cool sterility of the church.

My little spot reflects that casualness, so yes, it does seem a little honkytonkish. But no, "His Majesty" is not eating his breakfast on a barroom floor.

He's eating his braised chicken and creamed asparagus out of his Ming Dynasty dish on my honkytonkish living room floor. A house must be lived in to feel warm.

HAPPINESS PUSHING 80

It's droopy! The stillness not only cloaks; it's invasive. Thoughts of worldly matters are being pushed aside by the sheer majesty of the Creator's hand. Everything stock still, like a painting. If I could hear, I'll bet I could hear the Japanese beetles munching away on my green beans.

It seems proper that the young and the old find happiness in simple things. The years before being immersed in the scurry of life and the years after having survived it are truly the golden years. The years in between are so competitive, our lives so filled with the clutter of living, that simple things get overlooked. The little things we take for granted: the smell of honeysuckle, the rain, the very air we breathe, God.

Blessed by not being pressed, I'm able to sit on the porch and absorb the day and the elegant simplicity of it. Temperature and humidity are down in that zone where you don't need even a breeze. The sun and heat are cauterized by the cool waves of clouds rolling in from Tropical Storm Elsa. It's wondrous! I feel I'm at one with, or somehow part of, the hush, having no other ambition than to be here.

Happiness is not hard to find; it's just hard to see it through all the clutter.

TATER & ME

Tater and I recently celebrated our sixteenth anniversary. I remember it being such a happy day when we met. We hit it right off and went on home. For a month or so, I pretty much set the boundaries and laid out how things were going to be. I don't know exactly how or when, but after a while, that arrangement got reversed.

However, the first years were so wonderful! We learned about each other. He liked to yap; I didn't. For the next couple of weeks, every time he yapped, I'd grab him up and act like I was going to bite his head off. It worked pretty well. He still yaps, but only if so much as a shadow passes the door or if a pine needle happens to flutter down on the roof.

Since I didn't think there would be any, I was taken aback by the food issue. It took several months to figure out what he liked to eat. I found that out by spending $2,000 on what he didn't like. So now, to save time, I just fix chicken tetrazzini or pan fry a rib eye for him.

Then, there was the thing about him using the throw rug on my side of the bed because he took exception to doing his business outside in the dark. That one took awhile! After a few late-night foot washings and my quiet utterances of love and understanding, he finally decided to come clean. He let me know that when he stared at me with that death look, like my daddy gave me, I was to let him out. With that, our bedroom squabbles were over.
All in all, we now pass the days content with each other. Since he's gotten older, he lays on the couch all day and relaxes. I keep the house swept up and do all the cooking. Ever faithful though, he keeps one eye on the door and one eye on me. I understand and agree with watching the door, and I do appreciate his effort to contribute. After all, he lives here. But he's so suspicious! He must think I'm always sneaking a snack in the kitchen, for with the slightest movement of my hand toward my mouth, his feet hit the floor.

You know, when I think on it, it's like being married except a lot quieter.

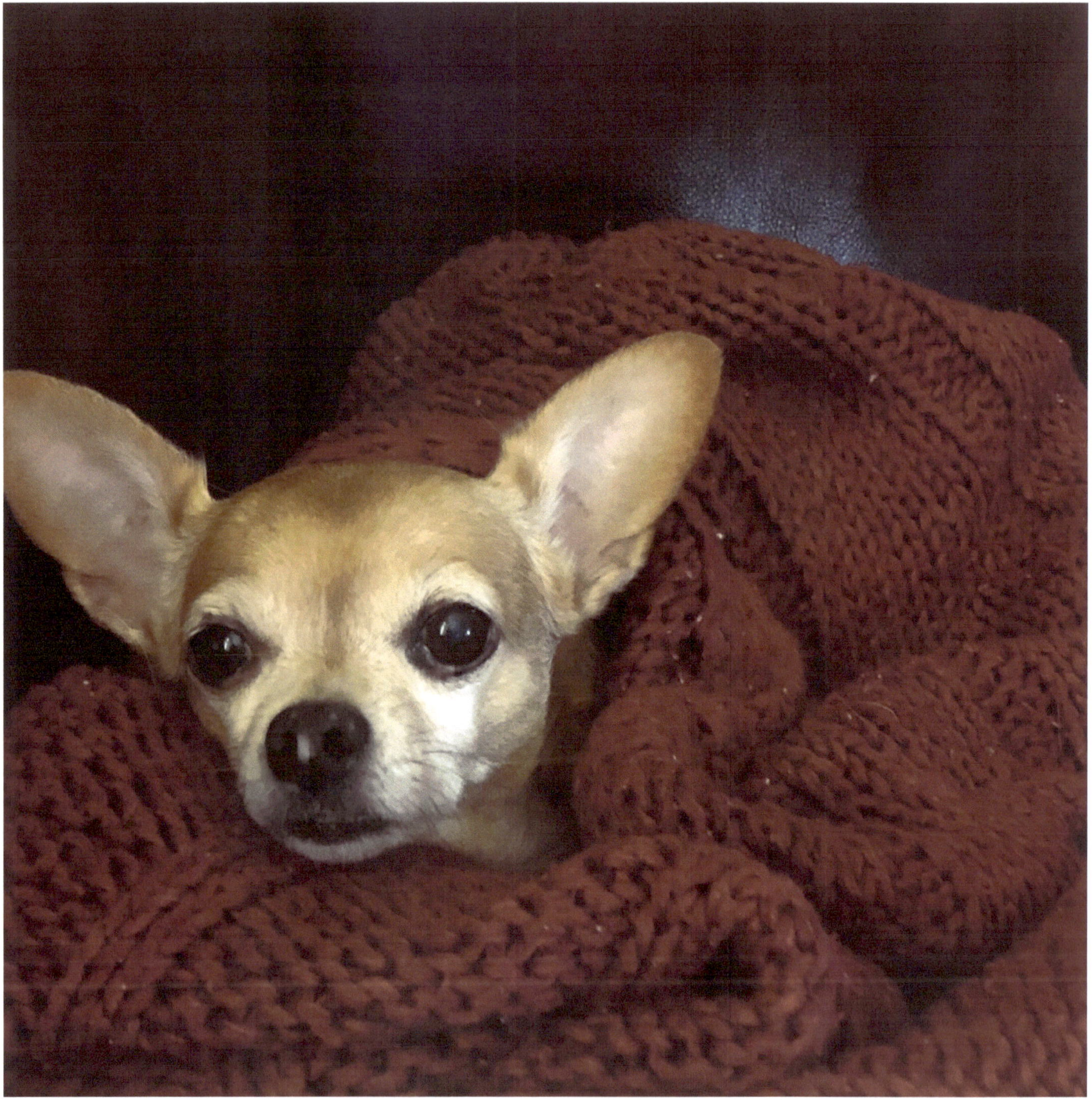

SILENCE

Your ears ain't open until your mouth is shut!

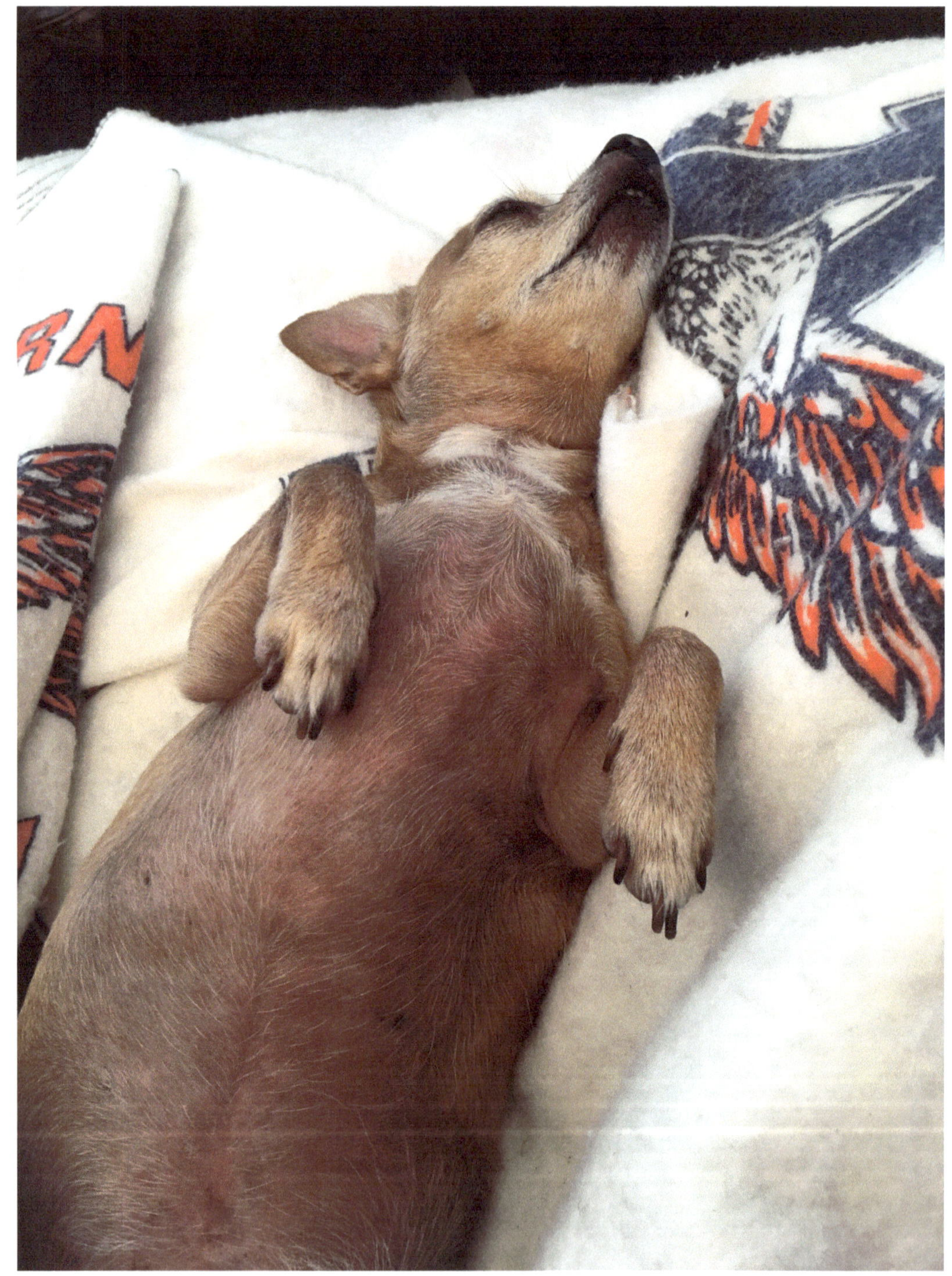

VIENNA SAUSAGE

Me and Tater were sitting on the porch swing in the cool of the evening yesterday, waiting for the rain to come in. The sun was down, but there were still streaks of blue in the cloud breaks. The birds were just about chirped out, and the frogs were chirping in. In other words, everything was copacetic in our world.

Then, without so much as a raised eyebrow, he let one ease out.

Oh my God! My body suddenly seized up, refusing to inhale. It was as though I plunged my head into a tank of water. I leaped up and fled across the porch, down the ramp, and into the yard, but it followed me, veritably clinging to my clothes. Oh my God! It was lingering over me like a cloud.

Let me tell you, mustard gas ain't got nothing on Tater gas. Bottled up, it could be used to break up riots, maybe even stop wars. A whiff of it renders you so helpless that it is impossible to carry on whatever you're doing without having specialized breathing equipment. Without it, the instinct to flee takes hold.

It was at least ten minutes before I dared the porch. When it was safe, I rushed inside, leaving him out for thirty more minutes. Like Joe Louis, Tater could well carry the moniker "Brown Bomber."

No more Vienna sausage!

GIFTS FROM THE GARDEN

"...and the joys we share as we tarry there, none other has ever known."

- CHARLES AUSTIN MILES, "IN THE GARDEN"

Understanding the wondrous machinery of Nature can most easily be approached in a garden. A flower garden gives us gifts for the eyes, nose, and spirit. A vegetable garden gives us all that and adds a gift for the belly. Both bring health benefits to the gardener.

Spiritual health is deepened by the satisfaction we find in the different flowers and their colors and in observing the Creator's delicate touch. Wondering if He had a reason why some flowers have more petals than others, why some smell of heaven and some don't. Was He just having fun?

Seeing for yourself what you were taught in school: the worker bees gathering supplies for themselves, all the while pollinating the plant to ensure its next generation. The arrangement of the bees harvesting pollen for their own use and "accidentally" ensuring there'll be more plants to make food for more bees is exquisite! How did this arrangement come to be? How could it not be planned? Seeking the answers to questions like these opens a pathway that leads to a nearness to God.

For mental health, it's simply uplifting! Nobody ever needed to see a doctor about feeling good. Feeling depressed is chronic in a society that's in a rush all the time. When we don't have a time for ourselves, to be still and consider things, things go south. That looking outward, toward light and hope, turns to looking inward, toward self-doubt and despair.

Gardening creates an opportunity to be quiet and reflect. It also provides a quick and positive reward for an effort that can not only be seen and appreciated but also eaten. It's no wonder that folks who tend gardens, especially those who farm, tend to be more respectful of the Way of the Creator than those who are reared up on concrete and steel.

"...and the joys we share as we tarry there, none other has ever known."
~ Charles Austin Miles, "In the Garden"

SAND MOUNTAIN TOMATOES

I've tried 'em from Texas to Barbados,
but ain't nothing better'n Sand Mountain tomatoes.

ON GARDENING

You know, it's easy to see how people who grew up in massive cities, those who have never gardened, slip away from a sincere belief in God. To never have experienced the wonder of planting a seed, cultivating it, and then feasting on it is sad. For if you buy what you eat from a merchant, your communion will be with the merchant. But if you grow what you eat in a garden, your communion will be with the Creator.

In my own case, nothing brings me closer to the Creator than seeing Him at work.

DOG DAYS

It's so still out here! Not even the whisper of a breeze stirs my Auburn flag. The bright orange and blue have been washed out in the merciless glare of the sun.

Laden with moisture, the air over the whole countryside appears as a thin fog. If bees are attending their rounds, they must be walking because it's too sticky to fly. Perching despondently in the trees, birds sit with their feathers ruffled out, their wings extended.

The dry and wilting corn has given it all. Fat ears with dried silks await the picker. Drooping trees struggle under a relentless sun, and dry, translucent leaves hang listlessly in the heavy air, waiting for tired limbs to pinch them off. Hard, knobby little tomatoes and a few forgotten pods of okra are all that's left of the garden. The corn, the critters, the trees, all of us are worn out with summer.

A bead of sweat just trickled down my nose and dropped on my phone. I'm going inside for a drink of water and breath of cool, dry, conditioned air. My critter friends and plants will just have to put up with these dog days until the Great Weathermaker turns on His air conditioning in a couple of months.

SUMMER RAIN

The pines know it! They sigh with the expectation of things to come. The corn knows it! Dusty leaves crackle with anticipation, feeling the message on the wind. The frogs know it! A dissonance of voices, rising from the bottoms, betrays the growing excitement.

Before the first clouds gather over the horizon, they know it! Rain is coming. Rain! That river that flows from the heavens, one drop at a time. It's the tonic that relieves the anxiety brought by blistering days and clammy, stifling nights.

Freckles appear in the dust as the clouds crack to shower blessings on the land. The pines dance and sing their breathy song; withered corn rises, reaching for the heavy clouds; the croaking in the bottoms becomes a chorus as the frogs sing out to welcome the first cool drops splashing through the ferns.

The long wait through dry, scorching days is over, and the earth is singing. The life force has been restored. God's blessing to us, one and all. Rain!

AFTER THE STORM

Sitting in my rocking chair on the porch, I'm watching a thunderstorm roll out to the southeast. The front has moved on, taking the wind but leaving the heat.

A lull, an unnatural silence has fallen. The once roaring metal roof is quiet but for a spattering of drops, a Morse code message, dripping from the pines. Not even the bees are buzzing. The lowing of a lonely cow whispers in the distance, ruffling the veil of silence.

Stillness, like cool spring water, seeps into my soul, bringing a timeless moment of divine peace. Somehow, I feel that I've been caught up in the flow of nature's river.

A breeze stirs the wind chime, summoning me and bringing me back to the porch. I feel the heat again as the mystical moment flows away. I'm not ready to let it go! I want to remain suspended in the thrill of timelessness and sense the nearness of our Creator.

I get up from the rocker, thanking God for the experience of the past few minutes, and stand for a moment, listening to the thunder as it rolls down Sand Mountain. When I step into the cabin, I feel like I did after the first time I kissed a girl ... I want to do that again!

THE DAUGHTER
I DIDN'T HAVE

Birdy was born September 26, 1958, in Birmingham and first saw the light of day as Kathryn Lynn Killough. I was 17, and I was there. At the time, my brother's third child's coming was a big deal, and my parents were thrilled to see their line extended. I won't say I was unhappy about it, but I was definitely nonplussed. What it really meant to me was that in the summertime, when my brother and sister came home, Kathryn's voice would be added to the nightly clamor.

My two older siblings had five squallers between them, and the little terrorists took disturbing the nights seriously. After a couple of days, they'd get in sync and start piercing the evening in shifts, with nerve-shattering screams. The constant wailing and the commotion caused by the adults tending to it put sleep at a premium.

Graduating high school in 1960, I went off to the Army, and while Kathy was growing up, I would see her on periodic visits home. I remember her as this odd little kid who stood beside the overburdened Thanksgiving table, eating nothing but Mama's yeast rolls.

During the days when I was chasing the neon rainbow, I moved to Nashville, and on a visit to see my parents sometime in 1979, Kathryn came by to see me. After a while, she told me she had been laid off from her job. At twenty years old, she was out of one of the few jobs available there and didn't have any plans. I invited her to come to Nashville.

My wife and I had a furnished basement, so she came to stay with us. It wasn't but a few days till she had the bus schedule and started riding into town. A week later, she had a job, and four weeks after that, she moved into her own apartment. A few months later, I hit the road with my band and lost all but sporadic contact with her again. Fast forward thirty-five years. I was in my third and failing marriage. One day, on the way south to see her mother, Birdy stopped by to see me.

A year later, with my marriage finally dissolved, I had to have emergency open heart surgery, and upon being turned out of the hospital, I was basically homeless. My family came to my rescue, and when I got on my feet, Kathryn volunteered to help me find a place to live. After a great deal of looking and not finding a house I could afford, we built a little cabin on property owned by her and her husband, Kevin.

My niece Kathryn became Birdy to me when I realized that, without children of my own, I started seeing her as the daughter I didn't have. After I got up and around, Birdy watched over me for two years, then nursed me through another year of MRSA that followed.

She sees that my bills are paid. She takes me to my doctor's appointments and sees that I take my meds. Since I have become hesitant to drive at night or for long distances, she has become my traveling companion. All things considered, she has taken up the role of a daughter.

I have a dandy little spot on her and Kevin's property, which is a few miles outside of Guntersville. My cabin, snuggled up against a pine thicket and facing a cornfield, is my story hatchery. At this point in time, Birdy is my first editor, aggravating me about commas. She's my critic who tells me when she thinks it doesn't flow. She's my first line of offense when something needs to be done.

If my family hadn't stepped up after my surgery, if Kathryn hadn't helped pilot me here, if my friends hadn't stepped up and helped me pay my bills, there would be no stories. Blessed I am and humbled by all the help I've received. Because of this support, I have a publisher and a book in the offing.

So Birdy, who started out as Kathryn, became Kathy to all in my family but my father, who called her Kat Bird. I shortened it to Birdy when she swooped in and rescued me. Now, the daughter I didn't have is frequently seen in public with a creepy old man who wears his britches too high.

SPRING

Fat robins have appeared in the yard. Tiny, green mouse-ear leaves are sprouting from the cold branches of the privet behind the house. Paperwhites and jonquils are pushing out against the chill on Sand Mountain.

As though a snow shower passed over, wild pear trees sprinkle the woods with their white petals. Yellow forsythias flutter like a flock of canaries in the wind; ruddy red quinces, the hope of Mama's jelly jars, glow in the morning sun. They are all beaming with the glory of spring.

Nature's reflection of death—the dark, cold, stillness of winter—is taking its leave and the thrill of life is returning. The light and warmth streaming from the heavens brings rebirth, growth, and the return of hope. It is impossible not to sense the joy of life.

The resurrection is here today, and I can see it and feel it! Is it any wonder that Easter, the celebration of Christ's victory over death, is celebrated in the spring?

THE P-51

I was sitting in my rocker, snapping my first little mess of green beans, when I saw what seemed to be a black dot out of the corner of my eye. Suddenly, I realized it was coming toward me. It quickly morphed from a dot to a BB to a baseball, and it was coming straight at me!

I lunged sideways, and when I did, it swerved, and something that sounded like a P-51 Mustang in a power dive roared through the door and into the room. It zoomed around, but boxed in, it made a crash landing up in the corner and skidded to a stop in the outriggers of Lucretia's web. Lucretia is my house spider. I gave her corner rights in exchange for taking out kamikaze invaders.

However, the Mustang, whatever kind of bug he was, must have been a nasty little bugger. He somehow struggled free of Lucretia's web and was lumbering into the air when I took a dead bead on him with the brass head of my walking cane. On the first swing, contact! He went from a big, bad bug to a BB to a dot. The last glimpse I had of him was just before he vanished from sight, apparently headed for Beulah land.

God! I'm working too hard … I think I'll go lay down.

LIVING WITH TUTORS

Every now and then, the Good Lord sees fit to put me through a remedial learning experience. He appoints various and different "tutors" to be sure that I "get it."

One of them is my dog, Tater. I'd been writing songs and making noises about love for a while, but the Good Lord decided I didn't quite have it down. So He arranged for Tater to come be my little pal. He stole my heart and helped me become better versed in the finer points of love and discipline.

While I was drinking coffee yesterday morning, a fly lit on my hand. When I brushed him off, he lit on the hand I brushed him off with. Then I don't know how long he walked around on my elbow before I felt it and slapped at him. He'd light, I'd brush him off, and he'd relight. I'd think he was gone, then he'd return and light again. After a few rounds of that, I yelled and called him nasty names, letting him know he had my attention.

It was unbelievable! That fly was either the bravest one God could lay His hands on or else he was in love with me. He seemed to think my swatting and my verbal abuse was some kind of mating ritual. Flitting around my head, he commenced to humming in my ear and touching my hair.

That was until his nasty little feet made contact with my forehead. That's when the war started. After slapping myself in the face and coming completely unglued, I jumped up out of my rocker so quickly, it tipped over backward. In and out of the bathroom we went, knocking over a lamp in the process. Charging after him into the kitchen, I spent several minutes darting around and flailing at the counters with the swatter. Finally, snorting and panting like a buffalo, I flopped on the couch. No doubt the fly was sitting on top of a ceiling fan blade, preening himself in satisfaction.

This morning, I sat on the porch and thought about it. My fly "tutor" did his job. He made me face the fact that the aggravation of a tiny fly can make me come unglued enough to lose control, shout obscenities, and trash the house.

So, OK, Heavenly Father, I "got it!" I feel the ruler across the back of my hand, and I'll try to do better.

But I don't know. When I think about the unbridled glee I felt when I finally nailed the aggravating little bastard, I suspect another tutor is coming.

THE PALMETTO BUG

The annual Medieval Fair in Sarasota, Florida, was held on the grounds of the Ringling mansion, and Darrel and I were playing.

There were suits of armor and statues of Greek gods on display. Huge stone vases filled with flowers had been placed around the expansive grounds. Some of the women were in period dress: full-bodied pastel dresses with puffed sleeves and dark, one-piece overwraps that laced up like a bodice and then flowed open from the waist down, much in the way of a curtain being pulled back. Men walked around in striped stockings that reached up to these strange bulbous pantaloons at their hip. Dolled up in frilly, puffy-sleeved blouses and pointy hats, they put the finishing touches on what was becoming an otherworldly day.

Acres of hibiscus covered the grounds where tea houses dripping with bougainvillea were tucked back in the trees. Stages had been placed at strategic spots amongst the tall, curving palms and huge banyans.

If you don't know about banyan trees, roots drop down from the limbs, take root, and become tree clones. This one, however, was kept trimmed, so the roots dripped down, reminding me of Spanish moss.

Our spot was in the shade under this big banyan. The stage was positioned such that when playing, we were looking out over Sarasota Bay. It was pretty dreamy ...

so much so that it was easy to overlook the little knot of people sitting in the small bleachers. I was feeling particularly snappy that afternoon, as I had just bought a new pair of tight-fitting white overalls and was ready to play.

It was a storybook spring day. Hot Florida sunshine, marshmallow clouds hanging in a sapphire blue sky, beautiful, manicured grounds with children running and playing ... just a laughing heart kind of day.

We broke down on our stuff, and after a while, enough people who were drifting by stopped until we had a nice crowd.

Sometime into our set, a roach bug the size of a fruit bat dived out of that banyan tree and directly down the bib of my new overalls. Everything went red, and I went wild! Mr. Bo Jangles didn't have a thing on me. I commenced to doing the St. Vitus dance the moment that thing latched onto my T-shirt. Being thrown into a pit of spiders couldn't have given me a worse case of heebie-jeebies. Something had to be done!

Leaping around and yelling at the top of my lungs, I somehow managed to put my guitar in its cradle with one hand while clawing at the galluses of the overalls with the other. I don't remember much, but Darrell later remarked that I was hollering and screaming obscenities so loudly, people clapped their hands over their children's ears.
A fruit bat was hemmed up between my T-shirt and the bib of my overalls, and it was steadily clawing its way south. Darrell said the way I was jumping around and flailing at myself caused the gawkers to draw back as if the stage had burst into flames. When I finally got the galluses undone and the overalls down, I snatched that thing off my shorts, flung it down and stomped it.

Suddenly free of the panic and somewhat dazed, I just stood there in my underwear, slack-jawed, until I heard Darrell hooting.

That roach bug had felt as big as a stone crab, and it had been crawling around in my shorts. I had to do something! I wasn't cool enough to just stand there and calmly pluck it out.

I won't describe the general uproar that ensued, what with parents hustling their kids away and all, but men getting naked in public seems to be frowned upon in Florida. I'd barely gotten my overalls up when security showed up.

With the help of the lady manager who hired us, we talked the cops out of any charges, but we were ushered from the grounds.

Ain't show business grand!

HOME IS ALWAYS BEAUTIFUL

Home is always beautiful to the one who lives there.

ANCIENT AROMAS

The smell of rain and the smell of freshly turned earth have much in common to me. They create a feeling of a primal closeness to the earth. The smell of rain on a hot, dusty day is a call to drift for a dreamer.

The scent of the freshly turned garden plot whisks me off to a time when I'd be with my daddy. We'd be following along behind four bottom plows, pulled by that old thudding John Deere, and taking deep draughts of the fragrance of upturned dirt in the Red Field.

The earthy smell of these ancient aromas spins me backward to a place in my childhood where time stands still.

JOHN WAS RIGHT

"Blow up the TV,

Throw out the paper,

Go to the country,

Build you a home.

Plant a little garden,

Eat a lot of peaches,

Try to find Jesus on

your own."

Gardening gives you time to think because a good bit of the time, you're alone. When you come to think about it, the water closet is about the only place we can be alone these days. Even when you're by yourself at home, what with the yammering of nonsense from the TV and the annoyance of the phone, aloneness is rare.

In the garden, you can be alone with the satisfaction of seeing purple hulls on the bloom, tomatoes ripening on the vine, and corn tasseling out.

Alone to stand back and look over the whole thing, to admire the symmetry, the straight rows, the clean middles, to feel satisfied that the effort is worthwhile. Alone secretly to marvel at the miraculous machinery of nature; to ponder how the obvious things are the hardest to see, like how dependent we are on the dance between the plants and bees. Alone to realize that none of it is coincidental, and it was set into motion by the finger of God.

The garden! Where the miraculous machinery of Nature is on full display. Where we can learn to be a little more thankful at supper when we pray.

THE HEALER

Every gardener knows that you cannot get what a garden gives you at a doctor's office.

THE GROVE

Rattlesnake Branch ran in a lazy "U" around the eastern edge of the red field. In most places, a giant step would get you across. It was spring-fed, and in the summertime, the flow was slow enough that stagnant water stood in pools, reflecting rainbow colors.

There was a stand of old-growth longleaf pines towering above that part of Rattlesnake Bottom, and it was crawling with fox squirrels. Papa said it was the only stand of old pines left in our part of the county, and to an eight-year-old boy, they were awe-inspiring. I had never seen trees so big!

They had shaded the grove so long that the only undergrowth there was scattered ferns and skimpy huckleberry bushes. Chattering squirrels made the only sound other than the whispering wind. Standing amongst the soaring trees on a squishy, brown carpet of pine needles spirited me away to my kid world of daydreams.

It was dim and shadowy in the grove, but here and there, laser beams of sunlight pierced the gloom and splashed on the carpet. Sometimes, I could see elves and leprechauns dancing at the edge of the spattering light. I always understood the elves were imaginary, but I saw them just the same. Looking up, through the loose weave of limbs and needles, the sun flashed and twinkled. It was a place of sprites and spirits, a magical place where time stood still. And though I never saw them, I knew … I just knew there were Indians in there and, like the squirrels, they were watching.

It became my place to go when I wanted to hide from Papa. No, I didn't go there to escape punishment; I couldn't hide from that. I went there because he'd want to put me to work, and I didn't care much for that. As the years passed, the elves disappeared, but in its eeriness, that stand of pines never lost its charm. I always felt a deep sense of peace when I went there. I didn't realize it at the time, but I've come to know that what I was feeling was the presence of the Lord.

The last time I went to the grove was right after I got out of the Army. Papa planned to cut the timber, so I gathered up my old .22 and my dog Crow, and we went to have a last look. Nothing had changed! I started thinking in whispers when I stepped across the branch. It was as if the trees were standing in a pool, undisturbed by the flow of the River of Time. The Indians and the squirrels were still watching.

Mesmerized by the cathedral atmosphere, I lingered and soaked it up. Several hours passed while I wallowed in the peacefulness. Walking back to the house with Crow, I felt content with the memories, the little kid inside me satisfied. For the first time, though, we were going home with two fat fox squirrels for Mama to cook. It was the last time she ever fixed squirrels smothered in gravy with her biscuits.

AMOS

Amos was a big, red mammoth mule. He and the dark, little jenny, Ruby, were the only two left over from the grand time of mules pulling the plow. The machines came and retired them to a life of hanging around the mule lot, an arrangement with which they seemed to be entirely satisfied.

I don't know what it was about the mules, but I was fascinated by them. I loved them! Even though I was a boy, I knew that their days as the heavy lifters on my daddy's farm were passing. Two model John Deere tractors appeared and took the mules' place in front of the plow.

Every spring and fall, Jesse Lee or Tut would take Ruby out and plow the garden. On summertime weekends, they'd hook them both to the old wagon, and we'd load up to go fishing at the gar hole. Most of the time though, the mules and wagon were used to take the hands to the field. As a boy, I helped carry water up from Rattlesnake Branch to the workers in the red field.

Every morning, I could hear them taking the mules out of the barn as I guzzled milk and stuffed syrup, buttered biscuits, and smoked sausage in my mouth. Mama must have understood, because that was about the only time she would allow me to bolt from the table without helping with the dishes.

I loved the way the mules smelled! I just knew that was the way it smelled on Tex Ritter's ranch. I loved all the gear: the collars, the hames, the trace chains, the way they looked, and the way everything hooked together. I loved the grinding sound the mules made gnawing the bit. I plain out loved the mules. They were my pals.

Most of the time, Amos and Ruby just stood around, swishing their tails and shimmying their muscles when flies lit on them. They fell right into the life of hanging out in the shade, watching everybody else work, especially Amos. I think, at one time, he was my grandfather's saddle mule because sometimes he would break into a single-foot when I was riding him back to the barn.

My grandfather rode a mule everywhere, until he got a motorcycle and finally, a car. Kit Thompson, who lived on Uncle Joe's place, told me one day that "Big Daddy" put Amos to the plow because he got to where he'd stop and wouldn't start. He laughed and said when Ol' Amos got to what he thought was far enough away from the barn, he'd just quit. Done for the day!

He balked that way behind Miss Nellie Grantham's house one day and forced "Big Daddy" to stay at Miss Nellie's house much longer than he wanted. Big Daddy had to build a fire under his mule to get him to move. Old Amos was pulling a middle buster the next day!

The mules were not troublemakers like that old gobbler and that hateful Muscovy Duck! That old drake tried to bite me. They'd run at me, all swelled up, thumping and hissing. One day, my daddy took his hickory walking stick and hit that turkey on his head so hard that he could never again open but one eye at the time. Broke him up from chasing me. Broke him up from chasing anything!

But the mules! The mules were so cool, they were happy to just stand around grazing and looking sublime.

Ruby was a little black beauty and a good plow mule. She was strong, quick, could geehaw with the best of them, and she wasn't fractious. When Jesse Lee finally started working the garden with the tractor, Daddy sold Ruby to the old man down the road.

Amos then became a perfect example of the Zen parable on "the value of being worthless" and spent much of his time being unconcerned about much of anything. He had made it to "mule Nirvana," and for his remaining years, had a private suite with a yard, plenty of fresh water, and me.

I kept the door to the corn crib open so he could nab an ear when he wanted. When he got it all eaten back to where he couldn't reach one, I'd get up and kick some down for him. Every Saturday, I'd talk to him while shelling corn to take to Mr. Braxton's grist mill. I don't know how many times I'd come to see him and find him just standing there, looking off in the distance as though he could see a group of jennies standing in a field of crimson clover. Old Amos was a cool old mule.

One afternoon, I got off the school bus to find a truck from the rendering plant down at Goshen backed up to the mule lot. They were dragging Amos out with a chain. It didn't seem right! They showed no reverence, no remorse, and that made me angry. It broke my heart to see old Amos manhandled that way. Mama was waiting, afraid for my reaction. She knew I'd be mad. But down inside, I knew that to those men, they were simply dragging an old dead mule out of his stall. They didn't know it, but they were dragging a lot more than that out of me.

With Amos gone, the time of the mule on my daddy's place was over.

A whole way of life on the farm slipped into the pages of soon to be forgotten history.

Maybe so! However, I shall not forget! I was born into the tail end of that era, and the little I saw made an indelible imprint on me. To this day, I still love the old ways, and I still love mules!

THE BEST LAID PLAN

When I was going to that institution in Tuscaloosa, my first cousin was at Auburn. His future ex-wife Jules came from a prominent family of horse people there, and one day when I was visiting, she asked me to tag along with her and some of her buddies who were going out to her daddy's farm to ride horses. I didn't particularly want to go fool with a stupid horse, but there was a bunch of pretty Auburn coeds and it was April.

The day we went for this ride was clearly made for love. Under a Walt Disney sky, bees were buzzing and birds were flitting around, chasing each other. Me, I was ready to do a little buzzing and flitting myself. I went to basic training right out of high school, so I was somewhat older than these girls. I figured that gave me an edge, and I already had my eye on a spiffy little redhead, who at first glance looked to be tender as little bird livers.

The scene was marred only by the knowledge that horses had to be involved in order for me to buzz and flit with these little fillies. Going along was not a question; it had to be done. I expected it to be a happy and rewarding outing and actually looked forward to it, even though I had a deep suspicion and distrust of horses.

When she asked me about it, I balked.

"I ain't crazy 'bout horses, Jules," I whined.

"Aw, come on! If they bother you that much, I'll give you Old Nell to ride. If you're still uneasy and you have a problem with her, you can just pull the reins to the right and she'll go around in a circle."

That sounded good, and it was persuasive. "Well, OK!" I mused absentmindedly, for I was thinking about just how GOOD that really sounded. My experience with horses was enough to know that a horse, once started, cannot be depended upon to stop. I don't care for that. I come from mule people. Mules will stop and can't be depended upon to start. I like that!

My mind was digesting her words. "Old Nell," she said, "I'll give you Old Nell!" I loved that. If I was going to have to ride a pea-brained horse in order to buzz and flit around the little flowers, I damned sure wanted it to be Old Nell. I didn't trust them jittery-assed horses.

Five ditzy sorority girls, me, and one other guy showed up at the family's plantation-like estate and gathered at the tack room. Jules had the farm hands bring out the horses; we collected our gear and started to saddle up.

A guy came ambling toward me leading an old mare about the size of a locomotive. An enormous hay-burning bag of gas, about 60 hands high, she looked like a bridge. I stood, watching him deal with ol' Nell and licking my chops. This was getting better and better! The guy was struggling such that I thought he was going to have to use a come-along to get the girth cinched up tight enough to secure the saddle.

Then, a lightbulb went off. "If I can figure out a way to get up on this old horse … there will be so many paths, trails, and cul-de-sacs to explore." I could see myself tying the horses and strolling down a honeysuckle-scented pathway while chatting up a sweet little Auburn farm girl. I had spotted that pretty redhead, who, by now, had spotted me back. "Oh, yes! Old Nell is going to do just fine!" She was so big and old, she'd lag behind and I'd get little Miss Muffet to do a little lagging with me. "It won't even look like a plan," I thought slyly.

After plodding up a lane between ancient crepe myrtles draped with Spanish moss, we crossed the road and gathered in the sunlight, waiting for Jules to unlock the gate. Miss Muffet and I were sitting side by side, our horses touching. I was putting my stuff on her. She was from Ohio and was so thrilled to be down "heah, in the South" that I just knew I could "Honeychile" this little bluebell into a little buzzing and flitting.

We drifted through the gate into a pasture, which I can't describe but as pastoral. Horses and a few cows were grazing in an expanse dappled with flowers. We were on the brow of a massive hill, which gently sloped down to a creek that was picturesquely lined with groups of towering cypress and majestic oak trees. The limbs and moss of the oaks draped down to about horse height. Underneath, they were worn flat as a ceiling from years of providing a shady gathering place for horses.

When Jules closed the gate, something came over ol' Nell. Her head, which had been drooping almost nose to ground, snapped up, ears standing straight, pointing like laser beams at the horses swatting flies under the trees. I snapped up too, suddenly filled with dread! With my legs, I could feel the wicked old horse's muscles bunching up, and before I could tighten the reins, she sprang forth like Seabiscuit from the gate.

The jerk was so sudden and violent that my head slapped against her rump. It was terrifying! I had visions of dying with a mouthful of dirt and a broken neck.

By the time I regained a sort of upright position, ol' Nellbiscuit was running full out, pulling for the trees with me and the saddle slowly beginning to rotate counterclockwise. My mind was a kaleidoscope of frenzied scenes, one of which was little Miss Muffet howling with laughter as she fell off her horse. I couldn't be concerned with it. I was too busy holding on.

"Pull her to the right!" Jules yelled. "Pull to the RIGHT!" I yanked. I pulled so hard that the old nag's head was turned to where we were practically looking each other in the eye. It was unbelievable! Me and old Nellbiscuit were looking at each other, and she was still ripping up the sod, hooves blindly thundering straight toward the trees. I had given up the reins for a double handful of her mane. Under the pounding, the saddle continued to slip to the left. My life began to pass before my eyes.

With my insides screaming from the hammering I was taking from Nellbiscuit, I found the courage to look up and recoiled with a sob at what I saw. The trees were coming toward me like a train, and the tree limbs were so low, I could see I wasn't going to make it. The old horse ducked and veered under the tree, raking me from her back and slamming me to the ground. The fall knocked the breath out of me and broke my glasses and my ego. The others came charging up and found me wallowing around, grunting like a hog, and jerking spasmodically as I struggled to catch my breath. I was hurt, but those twits must have thought I was dying. I heard "Ohh, no!" and "Is he dead?" mixed with a couple of gasps and one "Did y'all see that?!"

A hubbub erupted about going back, but I insisted they go on with the ride. They agreed when I assured them I was ok. Bruised, blind, and embarrassed, but OK. "Me and ol' Nellbiscuit are going to ease on back and wait at the barn."

I grabbed the reins and led her back up the hill. As we strolled through the dreamy pink of the crepe myrtle lane, I got to feeling better. After all, it was a beautiful day. Even with a damaged outer and inner self, it was a beautiful day.

We did ease on back to the barn, where I eased ol' Nellbiscuit into a stall, eased into my car, and eased on out of there. As I drove off, I was thinking, "Stupid horse! I had it all planned out. Mmmhmm. That tender little redhead, man.

Stupid-assed horse!"

THE WANGING DAY

It was hot. It was August, and we had been rolling for more than ten hours. After what seemed like an eternity on the shimmering highway, we pulled into the Flora-Bama parking lot at a quarter to five. Stepping out of the cool van into that sweltering Gulf Coast heat was a shock. The sand was white, the sky was white, the very air was white. That brick oven wind blowing in from the southwest didn't help either. It wasn't just hot; it was grumpy hot.

Because of a double booking, we were moved from the main stage to the tent stage, which made for an even more grouchy atmosphere. The stage was in a tent big enough to seat 400-500 people. The sides were rolled up, so basically, it was just a roof and much like a colossal convection oven. Sweat was cheap!

I was setting up my gear, concerned about how I was going to keep my guitar tuned in the heat and humidity We were all moving in slow motion and bitching with every step. All set up, I sat down and started tuning.

A young guy drifted in from the beach and stood not fifteen feet from me, swilling beer and watching. He was tall and so skinny and pale that I had visions of him rising from a tomb. The left side of his head was shaved and tattooed with "Hell's Angles" in black, with flames spurting out around it. (Yes, Angles!) On the right side, his hair was thin, bright pink, and hanging limply, like strands of spaghetti, almost to his shoulder.

I was paying attention to my tuner, so I didn't see him stumble up to the stage. By this time, John and Darrel had come out and were setting up their stuff. The boy said, "Hey!" Nobody responded. "HEYYY!"

I didn't know him. I thought he was talking to John, so I didn't say anything. After a few seconds of being ignored, he yelled, "HEY! Old dude! ... OLD DUDE!"

I looked up.

"Wang out some zep on that box, man!"

I didn't know what the hell he was talking about. "What?" I demanded.

"WANG OUT SOME ZEP ON THAT BOX, MAN!!"

Completely mystified, I looked over at John and Darrel, who were doubled over, howling. My fuse was short.

"Dammit! What the hell are y'all laughing at?!! What the hell is that nitwit talking about?!!"

John snorted, caught his breath, and, between guffaws, blurted out, "He wants you to play some Led Zeppelin on your guitar!"

"WHAT?!!" I screeched, spittle flying. "I don't give a shit what he wants! WHAT THE ... LED ZEPPELIN ... OLD DUDE??!! MY ASS!"

I sat my guitar down and, ready to chew sheet metal, took a step toward him. "WANG this, you stupid—" Just when I was getting into it, Darrel grabbed my shoulder, John grabbed my belt, and together, they pulled me back. I guess Pink Hair eased on out, but I'm not sure he didn't turn into a bat and fly away.

A waitress, who was bringing us water, saw all this. She sat the bottles of water on my chair, asked us to wait a minute, and went back to the bar. As we watched, she filled three plastic beer cups with Bushwhackers. Upon returning, she handed us each a Bushwhacker, gave us a little pat, and said, "Now then! Everything's gonna be alright!"

And so it was. The wanging part of the day was over, and the playing was soon to begin.

THE SAW

Have you ever heard anybody play a saw? A handsaw? As an aural experience, it's ... well, it's like the first time you hear a rattlesnake sing out: you get the heebie-jeebies and never, ever forget it.

I have a niece who seeks out and frequents places with live music. She sent me a video clip of a man, who, with a pianist, was doing what she said was a masterful rendition of a classical piece while playing a handsaw. She obviously enjoyed it, as she said she had seen him before. Out of appreciation for her thoughtfulness, I turned it on.

I immediately experienced something that affected me like an electric shock! It was like I touched a high voltage line. That sound made every hair on my body stand straight out. My skin! My skin was trying to crawl out the door. I slung the phone down like it bit me, and thankfully, the racket faded with the falling phone. I wanted to stomp it!

One time in the early '70s, I drifted down to south Florida where, down on my luck, I bottomed out. I was couching it with friends and dead broke. There was an off-Broadway theater in Coconut Grove, and when a touring troupe was in town, on the Monday in between a two-week run, they'd have a talent show. The prize was a hundred bucks, and I had to have it.

I practiced till the sweat from my sore fingers rusted the strings.

When the auspicious evening arrived, I went to find there were nine other poor souls like me who would kill for that money. Also, there was one guy from the troupe who was there because he wanted to have something to do. As the rest of us tuned up and got ready, he stood aside observing us with a snarky grin. We had to compete until there were two left who would do a final round with the guy from the troupe.

It finally came down to the girl with the banjo, me, and the guy from the troupe who played a saw. HA! A banjo player and a guy with a saw. Haw! Man, there was no way in hell I could lose ... I HAD this! I had never heard a saw played; in fact, I had never even imagined one being played. Consequently, I didn't know what effect it had on people.

That guy did. He fired in and played the beautiful "Sweet Leilani" on that evil saw. When he finished, besides being in a state of shock, I had a bad, baaaad feeling. Two little kids ran screaming from the room; some people clapped their hands over their ears; others stood and waved their arms around ... all completely undone! Sure enough, when the dreadful whining and wailing stopped, the judges were in such a state of mental distress and confusion, they gave the guy first place.

The second prize of $50 bought a set of maypop tires for my old car so I could get out of there. I took beating out the banjo player for granted, but I will be eternally mortified that I was beat out by a cheesy actor with that infernal handsaw.

PLAYING FOR JOHN

For most of my life, I have been a musician who makes a front-pocket living playing bars, lounges, and honkytonks. It's the kind of lifestyle you don't choose without the vague feeling you've got no other choice. It's not for strivers, who, like sharks, cannot stop without dying. It's for pickers who are satisfied to live in a smaller world where having fun making music is not so much a business as it is a primal force. It's for musical junkies who have a job at the parts house but can't envision living through a weekend without playing somewhere like the War Eagle Supper Club.

Guys and gals who live this way learn early on the difference between places you "want" to play and places you "have" to play. Musical hobos know that liking a joint is dependent, some 90 percent of the time, upon the owner or manager. A great many club operators view entertainment as a necessary evil and deal with it like a venereal disease.

There's not much problem in getting a gig at one of these places when you "have" to have one. They are the ones where the acts sometimes play for free. Conversely, those run by managers who love music and understand the lifestyle don't have any trouble booking the best acts their budget will allow.

I played the War Eagle Supper Club through four different proprietors over fifty-two years. I didn't play the last call on December 31, 2015, but I played during the last week. John Brandt, who managed it for its final thirty years, let me play in the afternoon or early evenings long after I started playing solo. The Supper Club was a band place, and John didn't have much need for a solo act. He booked me anyway. Also, he would open the club on Sundays to be used, at no cost, for benefits. He, along with the Coopers, staged dozens and dozens of shows to raise money to help musicians in need.

Working for managers like John was a pleasure and a relief. He treated everyone with respect and was so thoughtful, I sometimes wondered how he could do such a job. I suspect, though, that he might have felt about some musicians like musicians feel about some managers. A jerk is a jerk wherever you find one.

A part of my little orange and blue heart withered when the Supper Club closed. The memories, the friends, the playing songs for three generations of Aubies in that wonderful, dark old bar were over.

It is not just an honor for me, but a matter of thanks and pride to play at the gathering for John. One favor in return for the many favors he did for me and all the musicians who played at the Supper Club. I don't suspect you could find any act that ever worked there that wouldn't go back in an instant if John could open back up.

The charm, the magic of the War Eagle was not only in that dark, nasty, old building. It was mainly in the quality of the music and the attitude fostered there by John, Snapper, and the rest of the crew. I am daring here to speak for all the music people who passed through during his stewardship.

Thank you, John, for thirty years of making the War Eagle Supper Club a place where we could get "hot rock, cold beer, and no mercy" every single night … and sometimes during the day.

FLORA-BAMA.

ON THE DEATH OF BILLY RAY REYNOLDS

In my opinion, the industry we were part of passed over Billy Ray Reynolds! His life was not filled with the glitter and awards that much lesser lights have received. The attention paid to falseness in the music industry speaks to the charade of fame. Billy Ray Reynolds was a gnarled oak that stood quietly in the musical forest. That he has fallen quietly speaks to the integrity of his life, as he accepted the industry's ignorance with dignity.

I knew him for many years and was as close to him as the distance between us permitted. When I first heard Waylon sing "Atlanta's Burning Down," I wanted to meet the man who wrote it. God granted me that, and I will be forever grateful. His voice has been silenced, but Billy Ray's songs will endure. I shall never forget him.

HAND GRENADE SOUP

We had driven most of the night to get to Jensen's Resorts on Captiva Island, Florida. Reaching there at three a.m., we collapsed in bed. The next morning, we were like a pack of ravening wolves.

The Island Restaurant was about a half mile away, so we loaded up. It was about eleven-thirty in the morning, but the restaurant must not have been open long because there were very few people there. We jumped out and snagged a table. The waitress came and took the orders, and everybody seemed content to wait with their coffee.

Not me and LarryT. NO!! We had to have food right then or we were going to start throwing stuff! The soup of the day was chicken vegetable, so we each got a bowl, and when mine came, it was lukewarm, but it looked and smelled divine.

When I'm hungry, the first taste of whatever it is I'm having is sooo good. Well, this soup was good but not sooo good. At the end of savoring the first taste, there was this suspicious whang of a flavor I couldn't identify. Upon taking the second spoonful, however, it became sooo good that I sucked it up like a thirsty camel. When I finished slurping down my soup, I noticed LarryT scraping the bowl with his spoon too.

We finished eating, then back to the resort we went to shower, shave, and lay around for a couple of hours. Around three, we left for the gig.

Captiva is not the smallest island in the world, but it must be one of the most crowded. Where everybody was going at three in the afternoon in a resort area was beyond me. There was simply nowhere to go, and the traffic was so bad you couldn't get there anyway. It was like being in that Houston road rage traffic. Not only that, it was frying-eggs-on-the-hood weather! We crept and cranked the AC.

About a block from where we were to play, something in my mind reminded me of the sound of a dropping bomb in WWII movies. You know, a kind of a whistling whine and then "whump"?

Well, the "whump" took place in my lower abdomen.

"Oh my God!" I groaned. "This is what it must be like to fall on a hand grenade!" It felt like my small intestine was constricting, squeezing the … well, life out of my large intestine. I had that exquisite pain that renders you unable to think about anything else. It must have taken eight hours to make that last block. Oh, GOD!

I was holding back as hard as I could and sweating like a bull. My eyes were squinched almost shut so I could barely see. "Ohhhh … God!"

Leaping from the still rolling van, I tore out up the ramp. As I skidded around a corner, I ran into a guy who worked there. He took one look at me, pointed, and while drawing away from me shouted, "THAT WAY!"

Did you ever carry something so heavy that you had to strain every nerve to tote it? If you have, then you know about that overwhelming sense of relief that comes when you set it down … that long sssiiiiiiiggggghhhhh.

I washed my face and got the sweat and tears rinsed out of my eyes, and as I was leaving, I heard a big commotion. It was heavy panting, feet running, and what sounded like a grunting elephant seal. All of a sudden, LarryT, all 300 pounds of him, came tearing around the corner yelling, "GET OUT OF THE WAY!"

I jumped back, thinking, "The soup got the big boy too."

I know old LT could hear the reverberation of my cackling laughter as he lurched into the bathroom, jerking at his belt.

From that time on, we never again ordered any soup, chili, gumbo, or anything else that could be left in a pot overnight without demanding to know when it was cooked. Oh, yeah! Me and ol' LarryT … we know all about hand grenade soup.

CHICKEN ZEN

I didn't know what it was, but the first time I ever heard a zen riddle was on the school bus. A bunch of my cousins rode the same bus, and most of them were older than me. I was in the second grade.

When we stopped at Midway, my first cousin "Nugget" and a couple of older boys got on and sat down behind me. We'd gone about a mile when one of his friends leaned up from behind me and said, "Boy, you got any sense?"

"Uhh …" I stammered quietly.
He went on in a conspiratorial voice. "Boy, you know about chickens, don't you?"
"Uhh …"
"Where you think chickens come from, boy?!"
"Uhh …"

I just couldn't get past "uhh." Big country boys had a slithery way of tricking little country boys. Though I was only eight, I didn't trust him, and I was on guard.

"Eggs!" I finally blurted out with little confidence.
"Mmmhmm!" he sneered. "So, where did the eggs come from, smart boy?" And with a satisfied grunt, he sat back.

I was relieved. He didn't ask me anything else, and I'm sure he didn't know he was spouting zen any more than I did.

"So, which did come first?" I asked myself. So I twisted it every which way, and even at eight, I came to the conclusion that there was no answer.

If you've looked into zen, it's easy to become more confused than you were when you didn't know anything. You'll run into things like this: "What is the sound of one hand clapping?" To this day, thinking about these kinds of things frazzles my nerves. Same thing with the chicken and the egg. Damn! I don't know how I got off on this.

What made me think about chickens in the first place was Tater. Every day, we take the golf cart up to the big lawn in front of my niece Birdy's house, where I stop and let him jump out. I think it's necessary for him to have a little dog time. He spends so much time with me that sometimes I think he forgets about butt sniffing and all that stuff.

When he hopped out this morning, the grass was up to his chin, so he peered around until he spied the ginkgo tree. Then, if being a dog was ever in doubt, it came rushing back; he immediately went over and peed on it, leaving a message, I presume, to all others who sniff trees.

He knew I was watching because while he was doing dog stuff, he was steadily ambling toward the road. He appeared to think that if he meandered around looking disinterested, I wouldn't know what he was up to. After some minutes of wading through the grass, he wound up at the edge of road, peering intently at the other side, as if Seven Spanish Angels were calling for him. He sometimes seems to shiver with the desire to get across. (Tater's people are from Chihuahua, you know.)

Every day, he wants to cross it. Every day, without fail! He seems driven to go stand there, gazing wistfully. It's as if he is compelled by some mysterious facet of dogdom to go over there … on out, beyond the boundary of gravel and asphalt, into the realm of the unknown. It must be a powerful urge because sometimes he'll forget the rules, or more than likely ignore them, and put his foot on the pavement.

I sat this morning, watching for that foot to touch the road, wondering if we all have it … wanderlust, I mean. I've always had it! Tater seems to have it; caribou do. I think even orangutans probably want to go yonder and see what's in those trees across the river.

As I sat there pondering wanderlust and watching Tater, chickens came to mind. Well, I was wondering about wandering and it seemed only natural that I should wonder why the chicken crossed the road. About that time, I saw

Tater's foot hit the pavement, and I came zooming in, back from wandering around in the dimly lit corridors of my head. I barked a warning!

As we were riding back to the cabin, I was thinking about why the chicken crossed the road. It was pure zen. It's impossible to know why the stupid chicken crossed the road. It has no answer! Delighted with the recognition, I thought, "Zen." Immediately, I thought about the chicken and the egg.

Did I tell you about the first time I ever heard a zen riddle? It was on the school bus. A greasy teenager with bad breath and pimples on his face asked me which came first, the chicken or the egg.

Uhh ... have I already told you this?

THE SNAKE

It was warm for early spring, in the mid-80s. The redbuds and dogwoods were in their glory; the birds' twitter occasionally was broken by the call of a jay or the whine of a tree frog. The weather was perfect, and the warm sunshine seemed to thrill every living thing. Down in the pond, the bream were on the bed, and I was raking 'em in. It was poor boy perfection.

The day had gone down pleasantly. I even enjoyed mowing the lawn. My wife was busy doing a wedding with her plant business, so I fixed supper. We ate, went through our nightly routine, and turned in.

I was cradled in the arms of Morpheus, down in the unconscious nothingness of deep sleep, when at four o'clock, a calamitous explosion of crashing and screaming snatched me to my feet before I was truly awake.

"GOOD GOD!" I thought. "The house is falling in!"

Electrified with fear and apprehension, every hair on my head was standing out. My mind, though fuzzy, was working, looking for the door and—where was my wife?!

Abrupt as a heart attack, she burst through the bathroom door, wild-eyed and screaming like a banshee. Nightgown flapping, she charged past, knocking over the lamp, and literally skidding out the bedroom door. It seemed like an eternity, but all this happened in a matter of seconds. I was dumbstruck.

It was psychedelic! I shook my head as though that might clear things up and moved to see about my wife, who was on the couch in the living room, whimpering and shivering. I was so jacked up by the last few moments that empathy for her was way behind fear and jangled nerves.

"WHAT'S THE MATTER WITH YOU!" I shouted. "What's going on?! What happened in there?!!"

She looked up at me with such imploring eyes that I quietly sat down, gave her a tissue, and took her hand. She wiped her eyes and nose and whispered, "Snaaake. Toilet."

I drew back and barked, "SNAKE?!" Suddenly, I saw it all. It was like the sun came up. I jumped up, rushed to the bathroom, and stuck my head in the door. There was a snake all right, and its head was at least ten inches above the rim of the seat. It was sensing its surroundings with a flicking tongue, apparently planning to move on in!

The floor was covered with broken glass, so I went to put on my shoes. To keep the snake in the john, I planned to make it retreat with hot water, close the lid, and place books on it. My little darling had trashed her bathroom. She obviously did a lot of grabbing at things getting out of there.

Satisfied that the books would keep the snake from getting out, I returned to the living room. She had calmed down a bit, so I sat down and asked her to tell me what happened. Here's what she told me.

"The moon was shining through the window, so I didn't turn on the light. I sat down, but before I could pee, something cold touched my butt. 'OH, GODAMIGHTY!'"

She jumped as she relived it. "It might as well have been a naked wire. I screamed and leaped upward and forward, grabbing the shower curtain, but it fell in the tub along with the rod. When the curtain collapsed, I nearly fell, so I grabbed the towel rack. I couldn't believe it! The whole damn thing ripped off the wall. The holders came out and hit the floor. That left me staggering around with the bar in my hand."

She paused and took a deep breath. After a moment, she cleared her throat and continued.

"Anyway, I moved toward the door. Actually, I was high-stepping it, trying to keep my feet off the floor. I got almost to the door when, out of the corner of my eye, I thought I saw something moving back at the sink. I threw the towel rod at it, but missed, and I saw it hitting the mirror as I made it out."

When she had finished, my empathy had returned. The episode, the sheer terror, had beaten her and she showed it. By then, it was nearly five, so I fixed coffee while she showered in my little bathroom. At seven, I called the plumber, who came and removed a female cottonmouth moccasin from the toilet.

WORK A GARDEN

You are taught to say the blessing before you eat every day.
Work a garden and go to the table knowing what to say.

THE LORD WILL PROVIDE

Ahhh! A cool, fresh wind is blowing straight out of the west, and that grumbling off to the north means rain. I can smell it! Watching an approaching thunderstorm is a deja vu experience. I always get carried away by a feeling of wonder—that I'm standing before a force larger than I, a force beyond my control, which thereby puts me at its mercy. Over time, I've come to see it as the Good Lord teaching me respect.

Anyway, I came out this morning in my lounging britches, intending to cream some three dozen ears of corn from the garden. When I stepped out onto the porch at about ten o'clock, I was met with blinding sunshine, a scattering of flies crawling around on the shucks left from yesterday afternoon, and a scorching hot July morning.
Now understand, I'm passionate about my creamed corn, but these days, it has just about lost its charm. I may have reached the point of diminishing returns on creaming corn. I'm not cantankerous about it, but I resist having to do things I don't want to do, and creaming corn is a nasty business at best. As old as I am, I can still hear my daddy's voice, "Boy! Git out there and cream that corn like yo' mama told you to!"

Not having an excuse good enough for myself to accept, I just sat down on the swing and pouted. I didn't want to face the reality of creaming the corn or losing it. The thrum of hummingbirds, fighting at the feeder, was the only thing that kept the whole world from being sour. After a while, a rumble of thunder pulled me back to full consciousness.

Now the wind has picked up and the glare is gone. I can't believe it! A cool gust of wind blowing straight out of the west has given the flag a lift, causing me to stand up and move to the edge of the porch where I can see. There's a grumbling off in the north and that means rain. I can smell it.

I swear! I get a deja vu feeling every time I watch a thunderstorm come in. I'm going to sit down here and watch.

The corn'll wait till it starts raining.

THE DAY AFTER HURRICANE IDA

By now, you know that I do a good bit of sitting on the porch, and that's exactly what I'm doing now. I started out describing what a gorgeous day it is, but I can hardly type for soaking it in. After what Ida brought for the last couple of days, a nice cloudy day would have been just great. But to get a fairy-tale day like this on the first day of September, that is truly a spirit lifter.

Fall is in the air. Ida must have pulled the humidity along behind her to use in drenching Tennessee because it's wondrously dry. The sun is out, cotton candy clouds floating by, 'bout 79-80 degrees with a steady breeze from the west ... It's sort of like trying to describe Mama's fried chicken. It's hard to put into words. To that, add butterflies flitting about the late hydrangea blooms, the wind sighing in the pines, and you've got a fairy-tale day.

I took a picture from the swing so you could see it. I'm laying the phone down because I've run out of adjectives and I can't keep my mind on writing. I'm fixing to cut one of these Sugar Baby watermelons and get on with being blissed out for the day.

Wish you were here.

ON A RAINY DAY

There's something about a rainy day. A drizzly kind of rainy day. The soft murmuring of gentle rain on the metal roof engenders a creeping, hypnotic stillness.

Standing thick, green, and polished with water, the corn glistens under a pearl-gray sky. A languid breeze fluffs the trees, bringing a breath of cool air, washed of dust and smelling as only a rainy day can. Drops, haltingly dripping from the roof, seem to be in no hurry to splash the ground, intensifying the dreamy stillness.

With the sharp sound of gladness, the shrill song of a tree frog ruffles the droning from the roof and pierces the hushed day like an arrow.

I am spellbound and captivated by the feeling of being part of a Perfection. Worry and doubt soaked away, I drift into the day.

BELIEVING

Well, the God you don't believe in will still be here when you're gone.

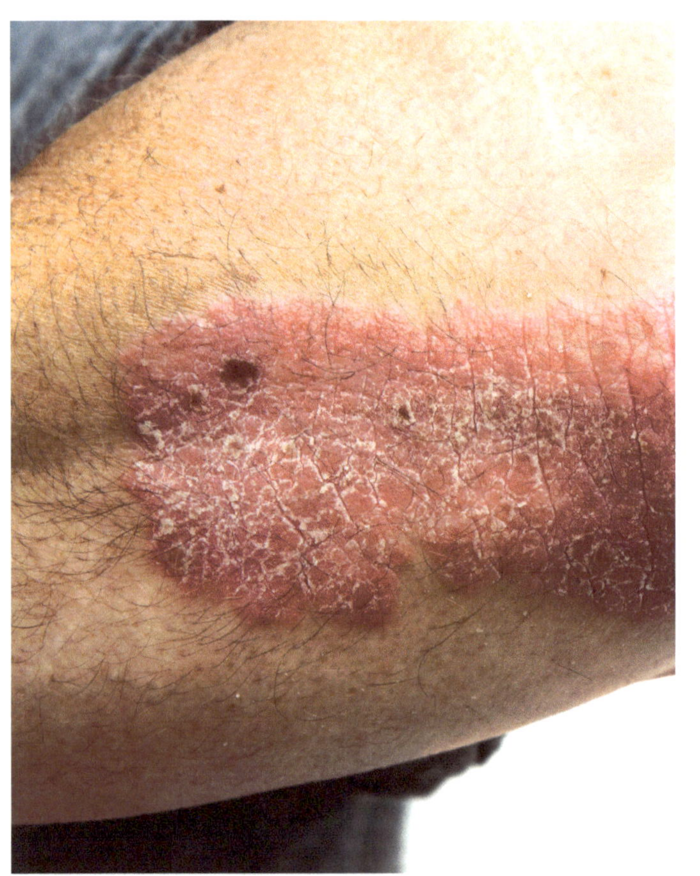

THE HEARTBREAK OF PSORIASIS

Maybe I just didn't pay attention, but it seems that all of a sudden, I see a lot of ads on TV about new compounds to help people who have psoriasis.

Psoriasis! The look and sound of the word conjures up images of tentative people with angry, flaky blotches on their skin. People squirming to keep from scratching in public. People whose coats and shirts are blooming with the white dandruff-like flakes. People who sometimes feel marginalized and embarrassed. People who did not catch psoriasis like the flu but who inherited it, like a bad heart.

Simply put, it comes from an overactive immune system, and you're born with it! When it can't find some intruder to attack, it turns on you, producing an overabundance of cells. This causes the splotchy, red, flaky skin and the accursed itching in the lucky few who are afflicted with it. The word "afflicted" was coined by a person with "The Heartbreak of Psoriasis."

About eight million people in the US have this curse. If you are one of the lucky ones (up to 30 percent of you), you are going to get psoriatic arthritis as well. On the upside, you'll never be bored; you will always have something to do with your hands unless you hire a personal "scratcher."

Most people don't know they have it until they're grown, even middle aged. I started having trouble with it when I was about six or seven. One day, my ears started itching.

Scientists say there are four forces in nature. There is 1) gravity, 2) electromagnetism, 3) the strong force, and 4) the weak force. However, there is one force that hasn't been fully measured yet, and that's the Fifth Force. The Fifth Force is a measure of the strength necessary to resist the urge to scratch. In my estimation, it's at least as strong as gravity. Don't tell me you haven't had the intense desire to take a piece of 60-grit sandpaper and get on down on that wicked and maddening itchy spot!

Well, when my ears started itching, I started scratching, and in time, the inevitable infection set in. After several months of hemming and hawing, that sadist who was masquerading as my doctor said I had a fungus.

"A FUNGUS!" my mother screeched, like she had just seen mushrooms sprout from my head. "A FUNGUS! OH MY GOD!"

That had a lasting effect on me. Pictures of fuzzy looking green stuff oozing with spores and growing in my ears haunted me for years. That misbegotten scum of a doctor told my mother that I caught it swimming in the creek. The no-good Bolshevik! Mama kept me out of the swimming hole until I got old enough to romp around away from home.

I was thirty-five years old before it was diagnosed. Steroid lotion has been keeping it beaten back, and I use "beaten back" as you would in dealing with a forest fire. It's not fun, and I empathize with all those who have awakened to intense itching in odd or private places. I empathize with those who have resisted going to the doctor. I know and understand the hesitancy that comes from suspecting you've got some disgusting ailment that you don't want anybody to know about, including your doctor.

Think about it. You can't go about telling people you itch! If you do, you will see a reaction that reaches across all cultural barriers and comes from so deep inside the human psyche that it's universal. It stimulates the urge to FLEE! We all know that a person who itches has some dreadful malady, and we sure as hell don't want it.

Those of us who have psoriasis do not wish it upon those of you who aren't stricken. Truthfully though, if you and I were standing in that line where this gift was to be assigned, and one of us HAD to get it ... I'd rather it be you!

So be prepared! If you are awakened one morning by a nuclear ITCH somewhere, like your ear, your nose, or your anus, you will soon feel the power of the Fifth Force.

Keep your fingernails clean, and best wishes.

SITTING UP WITH UNCLE TOM

I got to the house about six-thirty in the afternoon. "Cud'n" Bill was already there, and "Cud'n" Irby arrived at seven. My Great-Uncle Tom was living the last hours of his ninety-two years, and we were going to sit through the night with him. I was there subbing for my mother, who had sat last night then worked all day. It was October 1958, leaves were falling, and the weather was cool.

The old house reflected the sixty-eight years Tom and Aunt Molly had lived there. The walls of the rooms, which had long ago been painted, were sealed with smoke from the fireplace and years of exposure to life. A picture of Uncle Tom's father, stone faced in his Confederate uniform, and his mother, a dour looking woman dressed in black, hung in a big oval frame over the fireplace. The house was large, as were the drafty rooms. Built for hot weather, the twelve-foot ceilings made the dark, old house remindful of being in a cave. His wife and children were long gone, and the musty smell of their empty rooms was somewhat muted by the small fire in Uncle Tom's room.

We greeted each other, me doing the best I could to relate to the two older men. They were not Uncle Tom's boys but more distant relatives. I didn't know them very well. Our kinship was remote enough that I would have addressed them as mister if my mother hadn't called them cousins.

The sitters who were there when the doctor left all went home with "grave faces," according to Cud'n Bill. They passed along instructions on caring for our patient during the night and left a fresh pot of coffee for us. The first sensation I got upon walking into the room was the sound of his breathing and a hospital smell mixed with the faint odor of what I can only describe as death. He had throat cancer, and the area was open such that I could see his esophagus and the motion of his Adam's apple. The rasp of his breathing rose and fell, somewhat out of measure with his eight-day clock. Some minutes ticked by before I shook off the wave of nausea.

Every half hour, we were to drip a few drops of water on his tongue and change the dressing, which was a warm, damp cloth. When we changed the cloth, we were to spray it and the area of the wound with an atomizer. Uncle Tom had an IV drip going, which I took to be an exclamation point. Truthfully, none of us wanted to do it, so we decided to take turns changing the dressing.

The long night was broken up by small talk and nursing duties. I was only sixteen and didn't have much to contribute, but they had both been to the war, and I was hungry to hear their tales. With a routine established, we settled in, and the hours slipped away.

Sometime after four o'clock, a car pulled up in the yard. We had been told to expect Uncle Tom's youngest son, who was coming from California. The poor man had driven all the way in a VW Bug with very little rest. It was the first Volkswagen I had ever seen, and my gaping mouth closed only when the tall, thin man started to get out. He could hardly stand, so we helped him up the steps to the porch.

His name was Alec, another cousin I didn't know. We greeted him all around and brought him in. He stopped and stared at Uncle Tom for a long minute, then we poured him a cup of coffee and caught him up on the sad scene.

After visiting a bit, Alec picked up his chair and set it beside the bed. He sat down, took his father's hand, and said a short prayer. While he talked softly to the wasting old man, we sat quietly around the fireplace. The hush was broken only by Alec's tender voice, the clock, the occasional crackle of the fire, and that awful, ragged breathing.

Silently, the three of us sat staring at the fire, trying to stay awake. The fire and the droning sounds cast me into a daydream that I returned from only when something changed in the hypnotic rhythm. Uncle Tom had stopped breathing. We stood.

Then Alec stood, slowly turned to us, and said simply, "Papa's gone!" It was such a somber, time-stopping feeling that none of the three of us spoke. Alec pulled the sheet up and covered Uncle Tom. When we could process the finality of it, we expressed our condolences and called the undertaker. After he arrived, I went home, cleaned up and got on the bus, headed for school.

The events of that night got burned into my memory, and it visited me regularly for a couple of years. I had never seen a person die and had only once been around a person who was sick to dying. That night, coming face to face with mortality jolted me and made me really think about dying. And living!

Uncle Tom was dead, and it looked very cold and final. I had never thought much about dying until that experience, and it put me to being more attentive in church.

It's been sixty-three years since Great-Uncle Tom died, but I can still remember the smell of that room and the dreadful ebb and flow sound of his shallow, raspy breathing.

5462

LETTERS

They are different from telephone calls, these letters.
A letter can be held, seen, smelled, and heard with the eyes again.
They are different from telephone calls, these letters!
We don't mind the waiting.

DECEMBER WIND

The naked trees stand against a slate sky, rattling like skeletons in the wind whipping across Sand Mountain. It's only two o'clock, but the sun has taken early leave of work. Raw and gritty, the insistent wind pushes like an invisible hand.

Nothing is moving! The light is so dim I can see only the silhouettes of cows at the barn. The smaller critters are all burrowed down in their holes, huddled up in their nests, or curled up somewhere in the lee of the wind. Cracked with slivers of light, the leaden sky appears ready to fall on me as I step into the little cabin. Opening the door, it's as if I turned a page from the cold December wind to a warm room and the reassuring aroma of pintos bubbling on the stove.

I thank the good Lord for blessing me with the safe harbor of home and for the song in my heart. He is teaching me to let go of the past and look to the future with hope. I treasure these moments when I feel His presence. Moments of being right here, right now, where there is no sense of past or future. What a Teacher!

Let the wind wail ... all is well.

HOME

Be it ever so humble …

I've made several significant stops along my path. Had several homes! This little place is the first one that made me want to put a root down deeper than the frost line.

It ain't the home that comes to mind when I think about Mama, Papa, and the carefree years, but seeking it must be part of the mystifying thing that's kept me moving all my life. In the short time it has taken those hydrangeas to grow, it has become home. The hunger to move on has moved on.

It's small enough to keep reasonably clean and tight enough to hold Mother Nature's extremes at bay without swooning at the bill. It's as comfortable as an old shoe, and it's so far up the country, I ought to paint my mailbox blue. To leave, something has to pull me out, and when I'm out, something pulls me to get back.

Sometimes it's hard to keep my spirits up, what with being a short timer and all, but sitting on the porch, getting to see the sun come and go, with the wind whispering in the pines, I feel the certainty of that line in the Twenty-third Psalm, "He restoreth my soul."

God is so generous with His blessings. It's a happy little place for me, and hopefully, it is where I will be when the bell rings.

… there's no place like home.

SUNDOWN COMMUNION

The sun is going down! Splashes of reds, golds, and purples streak through the sheep-like clouds. But for the intermittent growl of a tractor coming with the evening breeze and the twitter of birds, the day is quietly coming to a close. The occasional chirr of a tree frog and the subliminal rise of voices from the grass envelop me, as the calming sounds of the evening release me from the clamor of the day.

Three cattle egrets glide across the cornfield, angling for their roost. The sun is fading, but the moon is already well up in the southeast. I can hear the wind in the pines, and I think of angels whispering to each other.

Sitting on the porch on evenings like this, I seem to become absorbed by what's going on around me. That seems to happen only when there are no competitive thoughts goading me for attention. It's as if I've been quietly written into the script of this great production, that I've become part of it, not just a witness to it. I am overcome by a feeling of awe and my own smallness in the majesty of creation.

As I sit here, gazing across the cornfield, watching the night absorb the day, a divine silence drowns out all but the whispering angels. The Creator is near.

www.ingramcontent.com/pod-product-compliance
Lightning Source LLC
Chambersburg PA
CBHW041925180726
48295CB00003B/78